# Ordinal N



1st first

2nd second

3rd third

4th fourth

5th fifth

6th sixth

7th seventh

8th eighth

9th ninth

10th tenth

11th eleventh

12th twelfth

20th twentieth

100th hundredth

1000th thousandth

*A handbook of tables and other measures which will be a useful source of quick and easy reference in any household. This book is also ideal for a child who is ready to learn multiplication tables.*

---

## Contents



---


*Acknowledgments:*
The author and publishers would like to thank the following for their valuable assistance during the compiling of this book: Loughborough D.I.Y. and Building Supplies, the Clothing and Footwear Institute, Shoe and Allied Trades Research Association and B.S.C. Footwear Ltd.

Published by Ladybird Books Ltd Loughborough Leicestershire UK
Ladybird Books Inc Lewiston Maine 04240 USA

# the Ladybird book of TABLES

## and other measures

*compiled by* DOROTHY PAULL
*designed and illustrated*
*by* HURLSTON DESIGN LTD

Ladybird Books

0 × 2 = 0

1 × 2 = 2

2 × 2 = 4

3 × 2 = 6

4 × 2 = 8

5 × 2 = 10

6 × 2 = 12

7 × 2 = 14

8 × 2 = 16

9 × 2 = 18

10 × 2 = 20

11 × 2 = 22

12 × 2 = 24

| | | | | | | | | | |
|---|---|---|---|---|---|---|---|---|---|
| 1 | 2 | 3 | 4 | 5 | 6 | 7 | 8 | 9 | 10 |
| 11 | 12 | 13 | 14 | 15 | 16 | 17 | 18 | 19 | 20 |
| 21 | 22 | 23 | 24 | 25 | 26 | 27 | 28 | 29 | 30 |
| 31 | 32 | 33 | 34 | 35 | 36 | 37 | 38 | 39 | 40 |
| 41 | 42 | 43 | 44 | 45 | 46 | 47 | 48 | 49 | 50 |
| 51 | 52 | 53 | 54 | 55 | 56 | 57 | 58 | 59 | 60 |
| 61 | 62 | 63 | 64 | 65 | 66 | 67 | 68 | 69 | 70 |
| 71 | 72 | 73 | 74 | 75 | 76 | 77 | 78 | 79 | 80 |
| 81 | 82 | 83 | 84 | 85 | 86 | 87 | 88 | 89 | 90 |
| 91 | 92 | 93 | 94 | 95 | 96 | 97 | 98 | 99 | 100 |

**Words:** **2 two** **2nd second**

| | |
|---|---|
| double | two times as much |
| pair | two matching items |
| bicycle | two-wheeled cycle |
| tandem | cycle for two people |
| duet | song or music for two voices or instruments |
| twins | two children born at the same birth |
| couplet | two lines of verse |
| twice | two times |

# 3 times table

0 × 3 = 0
1 × 3 = 3
2 × 3 = 6
3 × 3 = 9
4 × 3 = 12
5 × 3 = 15
6 × 3 = 18
7 × 3 = 21
8 × 3 = 24
9 × 3 = 27
10 × 3 = 30
11 × 3 = 33
12 × 3 = 36

| 1 | 2 | 3 | 4 | 5 | 6 | 7 | 8 | 9 | 10 |
|---|---|---|---|---|---|---|---|---|---|
| 11 | 12 | 13 | 14 | 15 | 16 | 17 | 18 | 19 | 20 |
| 21 | 22 | 23 | 24 | 25 | 26 | 27 | 28 | 29 | 30 |
| 31 | 32 | 33 | 34 | 35 | 36 | 37 | 38 | 39 | 40 |
| 41 | 42 | 43 | 44 | 45 | 46 | 47 | 48 | 49 | 50 |
| 51 | 52 | 53 | 54 | 55 | 56 | 57 | 58 | 59 | 60 |
| 61 | 62 | 63 | 64 | 65 | 66 | 67 | 68 | 69 | 70 |
| 71 | 72 | 73 | 74 | 75 | 76 | 77 | 78 | 79 | 80 |
| 81 | 82 | 83 | 84 | 85 | 86 | 87 | 88 | 89 | 90 |
| 91 | 92 | 93 | 94 | 95 | 96 | 97 | 98 | 99 | 100 |

**Words:** **3 three** **3rd third**

| | |
|---|---|
| **trio** | three people singing or playing instruments |
| **triplets** | three children born at the same birth |
| **tripod** | a stand or anything on three feet or legs |
| **tricycle** | three-wheeled cycle |
| **trilogy** | three part play or book |
| **treble**<br>**triple** | three times as much; threefold |
| **triangle** | a three-sided plane shape |

0 × 4 = 0

1 × 4 = 4

2 × 4 = 8

3 × 4 = 12

4 × 4 = 16

5 × 4 = 20

6 × 4 = 24

7 × 4 = 28

8 × 4 = 32

9 × 4 = 36

10 × 4 = 40

11 × 4 = 44

12 × 4 = 48

| 1 | 2 | 3 | 4 | 5 | 6 | 7 | 8 | 9 | 10 |
|---|---|---|---|---|---|---|---|---|---|
| 11 | 12 | 13 | 14 | 15 | 16 | 17 | 18 | 19 | 20 |
| 21 | 22 | 23 | 24 | 25 | 26 | 27 | 28 | 29 | 30 |
| 31 | 32 | 33 | 34 | 35 | 36 | 37 | 38 | 39 | 40 |
| 41 | 42 | 43 | 44 | 45 | 46 | 47 | 48 | 49 | 50 |
| 51 | 52 | 53 | 54 | 55 | 56 | 57 | 58 | 59 | 60 |
| 61 | 62 | 63 | 64 | 65 | 66 | 67 | 68 | 69 | 70 |
| 71 | 72 | 73 | 74 | 75 | 76 | 77 | 78 | 79 | 80 |
| 81 | 82 | 83 | 84 | 85 | 86 | 87 | 88 | 89 | 90 |
| 91 | 92 | 93 | 94 | 95 | 96 | 97 | 98 | 99 | 100 |

**Words: 4 four 4th fourth**

| | |
|---|---|
| quartet | four people singing or playing instruments |
| quarter | one of four equal parts of a whole |
| quadruped | a four-legged animal |
| quadrant | a fourth part or quarter of a circle |
| quadruplets or quads | four children born at the same birth |
| square | a four-sided plane shape |

# 5 times table

0 × 5 = 0

1 × 5 = 5

2 × 5 = 10

3 × 5 = 15

4 × 5 = 20

5 × 5 = 25

6 × 5 = 30

7 × 5 = 35

8 × 5 = 40

9 × 5 = 45

10 × 5 = 50

11 × 5 = 55

12 × 5 = 60

| 1 | 2 | 3 | 4 | 5 | 6 | 7 | 8 | 9 | 10 |
|---|---|---|---|---|---|---|---|---|---|
| 11 | 12 | 13 | 14 | 15 | 16 | 17 | 18 | 19 | 20 |
| 21 | 22 | 23 | 24 | 25 | 26 | 27 | 28 | 29 | 30 |
| 31 | 32 | 33 | 34 | 35 | 36 | 37 | 38 | 39 | 40 |
| 41 | 42 | 43 | 44 | 45 | 46 | 47 | 48 | 49 | 50 |
| 51 | 52 | 53 | 54 | 55 | 56 | 57 | 58 | 59 | 60 |
| 61 | 62 | 63 | 64 | 65 | 66 | 67 | 68 | 69 | 70 |
| 71 | 72 | 73 | 74 | 75 | 76 | 77 | 78 | 79 | 80 |
| 81 | 82 | 83 | 84 | 85 | 86 | 87 | 88 | 89 | 90 |
| 91 | 92 | 93 | 94 | 95 | 96 | 97 | 98 | 99 | 100 |

**Words:** **5 five** **5th fifth**

| | |
|---|---|
| quintet | five people singing or playing instruments |
| quintuplets or quins | five children born at the same birth |
| pentagon | a five-sided plane shape |
| pentathlon | athletic contest with five events for each competitor |
| quintuple | five times as much |
| quinquennial | happening once every five years |

0 × 6 = 0

1 × 6 = 6

2 × 6 = 12

3 × 6 = 18

4 × 6 = 24

5 × 6 = 30

6 × 6 = 36

7 × 6 = 42

8 × 6 = 48

9 × 6 = 54

10 × 6 = 60

11 × 6 = 66

12 × 6 = 72

| 1 | 2 | 3 | 4 | 5 | 6 | 7 | 8 | 9 | 10 |
|---|---|---|---|---|---|---|---|---|---|
| 11 | 12 | 13 | 14 | 15 | 16 | 17 | 18 | 19 | 20 |
| 21 | 22 | 23 | 24 | 25 | 26 | 27 | 28 | 29 | 30 |
| 31 | 32 | 33 | 34 | 35 | 36 | 37 | 38 | 39 | 40 |
| 41 | 42 | 43 | 44 | 45 | 46 | 47 | 48 | 49 | 50 |
| 51 | 52 | 53 | 54 | 55 | 56 | 57 | 58 | 59 | 60 |
| 61 | 62 | 63 | 64 | 65 | 66 | 67 | 68 | 69 | 70 |
| 71 | 72 | 73 | 74 | 75 | 76 | 77 | 78 | 79 | 80 |
| 81 | 82 | 83 | 84 | 85 | 86 | 87 | 88 | 89 | 90 |
| 91 | 92 | 93 | 94 | 95 | 96 | 97 | 98 | 99 | 100 |

**Words:** **6 six** **6th sixth**

| | |
|---|---|
| **sextet** | six people singing or playing instruments |
| **sextuplets** | six children born at the same birth |
| **sextant** | a sixth part of a circle; an instrument for measuring angles and distances |
| **hexagon** | a six-sided plane shape |
| **sextuple** | six times as much |

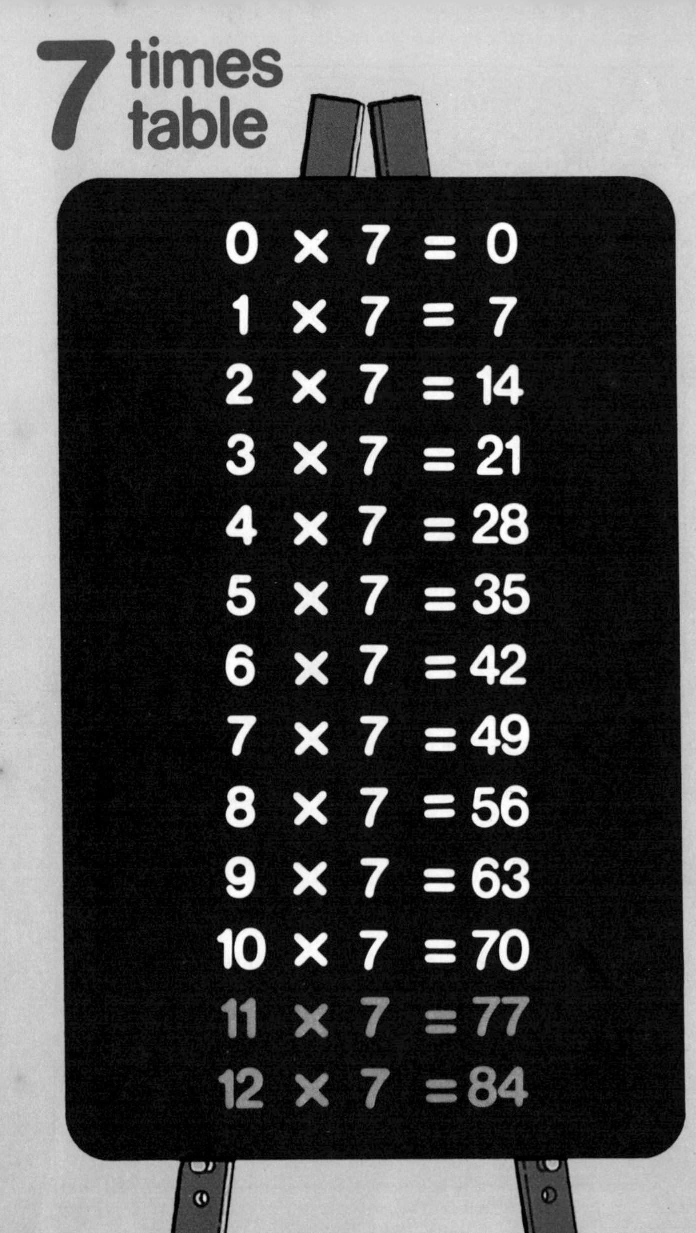
7 times table
0 × 7 = 0
1 × 7 = 7
2 × 7 = 14
3 × 7 = 21
4 × 7 = 28
5 × 7 = 35
6 × 7 = 42
7 × 7 = 49
8 × 7 = 56
9 × 7 = 63
10 × 7 = 70
11 × 7 = 77
12 × 7 = 84

| 1 | 2 | 3 | 4 | 5 | 6 | 7 | 8 | 9 | 10 |
|---|---|---|---|---|---|---|---|---|---|
| 11 | 12 | 13 | 14 | 15 | 16 | 17 | 18 | 19 | 20 |
| 21 | 22 | 23 | 24 | 25 | 26 | 27 | 28 | 29 | 30 |
| 31 | 32 | 33 | 34 | 35 | 36 | 37 | 38 | 39 | 40 |
| 41 | 42 | 43 | 44 | 45 | 46 | 47 | 48 | 49 | 50 |
| 51 | 52 | 53 | 54 | 55 | 56 | 57 | 58 | 59 | 60 |
| 61 | 62 | 63 | 64 | 65 | 66 | 67 | 68 | 69 | 70 |
| 71 | 72 | 73 | 74 | 75 | 76 | 77 | 78 | 79 | 80 |
| 81 | 82 | 83 | 84 | 85 | 86 | 87 | 88 | 89 | 90 |
| 91 | 92 | 93 | 94 | 95 | 96 | 97 | 98 | 99 | 100 |

**Words:** **7 seven** **7th seventh**

| | |
|---|---|
| **heptagon** | a seven-sided plane shape |
| **September** | in Roman times, the 7th month of the year |
| **septet** | seven people singing or playing instruments |
| **septuagen-arian** | a person of 70 to 80 years old |

$0 \times 8 = 0$

$1 \times 8 = 8$

$2 \times 8 = 16$

$3 \times 8 = 24$

$4 \times 8 = 32$

$5 \times 8 = 40$

$6 \times 8 = 48$

$7 \times 8 = 56$

$8 \times 8 = 64$

$9 \times 8 = 72$

$10 \times 8 = 80$

$11 \times 8 = 88$

$12 \times 8 = 96$

| | | | | | | | | | |
|---|---|---|---|---|---|---|---|---|---|
| 1 | 2 | 3 | 4 | 5 | 6 | 7 | 8 | 9 | 10 |
| 11 | 12 | 13 | 14 | 15 | 16 | 17 | 18 | 19 | 20 |
| 21 | 22 | 23 | 24 | 25 | 26 | 27 | 28 | 29 | 30 |
| 31 | 32 | 33 | 34 | 35 | 36 | 37 | 38 | 39 | 40 |
| 41 | 42 | 43 | 44 | 45 | 46 | 47 | 48 | 49 | 50 |
| 51 | 52 | 53 | 54 | 55 | 56 | 57 | 58 | 59 | 60 |
| 61 | 62 | 63 | 64 | 65 | 66 | 67 | 68 | 69 | 70 |
| 71 | 72 | 73 | 74 | 75 | 76 | 77 | 78 | 79 | 80 |
| 81 | 82 | 83 | 84 | 85 | 86 | 87 | 88 | 89 | 90 |
| 91 | 92 | 93 | 94 | 95 | 96 | 97 | 98 | 99 | 100 |

**Words:** **8 eight** **8th eighth**

| | |
|---|---|
| **octet** | eight people singing or playing instruments |
| **octagon** | an eight-sided plane shape |
| **octave** | a group of eight musical notes |
| **octopus** | a sea creature with eight tentacles |
| **octogen-arian** | a person of 80 to 90 years old |
| **October** | in Roman times, the 8th month of the year |

0 × 9 = 0
1 × 9 = 9
2 × 9 = 18
3 × 9 = 27
4 × 9 = 36
5 × 9 = 45
6 × 9 = 54
7 × 9 = 63
8 × 9 = 72
9 × 9 = 81
10 × 9 = 90
11 × 9 = 99
12 × 9 = 108

| | | | | | | | | | |
|---|---|---|---|---|---|---|---|---|---|
| 1 | 2 | 3 | 4 | 5 | 6 | 7 | 8 | 9 | 10 |
| 11 | 12 | 13 | 14 | 15 | 16 | 17 | 18 | 19 | 20 |
| 21 | 22 | 23 | 24 | 25 | 26 | 27 | 28 | 29 | 30 |
| 31 | 32 | 33 | 34 | 35 | 36 | 37 | 38 | 39 | 40 |
| 41 | 42 | 43 | 44 | 45 | 46 | 47 | 48 | 49 | 50 |
| 51 | 52 | 53 | 54 | 55 | 56 | 57 | 58 | 59 | 60 |
| 61 | 62 | 63 | 64 | 65 | 66 | 67 | 68 | 69 | 70 |
| 71 | 72 | 73 | 74 | 75 | 76 | 77 | 78 | 79 | 80 |
| 81 | 82 | 83 | 84 | 85 | 86 | 87 | 88 | 89 | 90 |
| 91 | 92 | 93 | 94 | 95 | 96 | 97 | 98 | 99 | 100 |

**Words:** **9 nine** **9th ninth**

**nonet** — nine people singing or playing instruments

**nonagenarian** — a person of 90 to 100 years old

**November** — in Roman times, the 9th month of the year

0 × 10 = 0
1 × 10 = 10
2 × 10 = 20
3 × 10 = 30
4 × 10 = 40
5 × 10 = 50
6 × 10 = 60
7 × 10 = 70
8 × 10 = 80
9 × 10 = 90
10 × 10 = 100
11 × 10 = 110
12 × 10 = 120

| | | | | | | | | | |
|---|---|---|---|---|---|---|---|---|---|
| 1 | 2 | 3 | 4 | 5 | 6 | 7 | 8 | 9 | 10 |
| 11 | 12 | 13 | 14 | 15 | 16 | 17 | 18 | 19 | 20 |
| 21 | 22 | 23 | 24 | 25 | 26 | 27 | 28 | 29 | 30 |
| 31 | 32 | 33 | 34 | 35 | 36 | 37 | 38 | 39 | 40 |
| 41 | 42 | 43 | 44 | 45 | 46 | 47 | 48 | 49 | 50 |
| 51 | 52 | 53 | 54 | 55 | 56 | 57 | 58 | 59 | 60 |
| 61 | 62 | 63 | 64 | 65 | 66 | 67 | 68 | 69 | 70 |
| 71 | 72 | 73 | 74 | 75 | 76 | 77 | 78 | 79 | 80 |
| 81 | 82 | 83 | 84 | 85 | 86 | 87 | 88 | 89 | 90 |
| 91 | 92 | 93 | 94 | 95 | 96 | 97 | 98 | 99 | 100 |

**Words:** **10 ten** **10th tenth**

**decade** ten years
**decimal** of tenths; counting in tens
**decagon** a ten-sided plane shape
**decahedron** a regular solid with ten faces
**decathlon** an athletic contest with ten events for each competitor
**December** in Roman times, the 10th month of the year

$0 \times 11 = 0$

$1 \times 11 = 11$

$2 \times 11 = 22$

$3 \times 11 = 33$

$4 \times 11 = 44$

$5 \times 11 = 55$

$6 \times 11 = 66$

$7 \times 11 = 77$

$8 \times 11 = 88$

$9 \times 11 = 99$

$10 \times 11 = 110$

$11 \times 11 = 121$

$12 \times 11 = 132$

# 12 times table

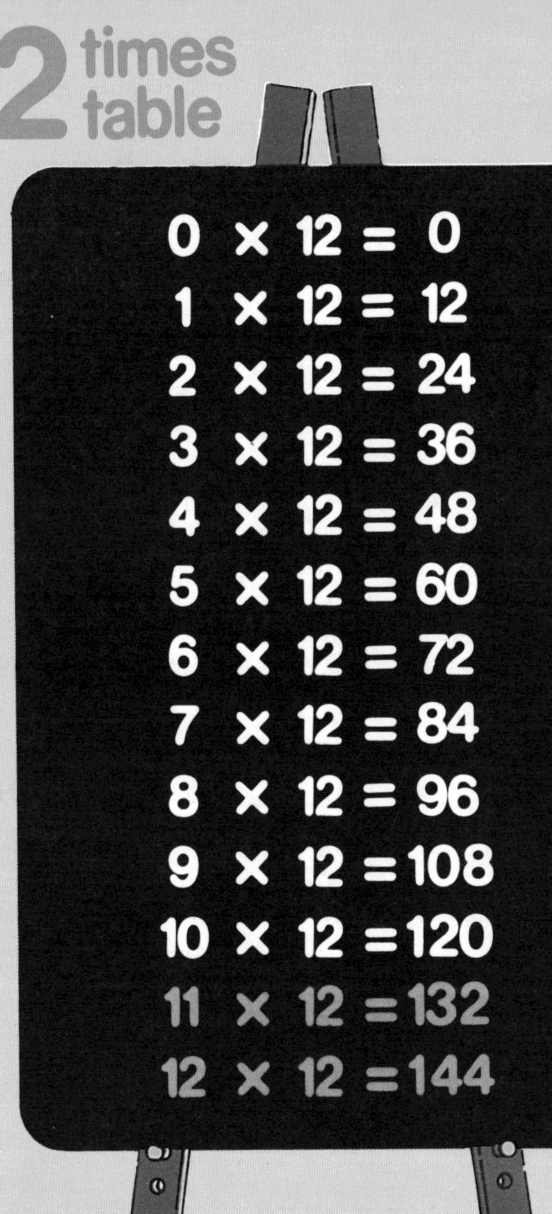

# Fractions and Decimals

| Fractions *Parts of a whole* | Decimals *Number shown in tenths* |
|---|---|
| $\frac{1}{10}$ | 0.1 |
| $\frac{1}{100}$ | 0.01 |
| $\frac{1}{1000}$ | 0.001 |
| $\frac{1}{4}$ | 0.25 |
| $\frac{1}{2}$ | 0.50 |
| $\frac{3}{4}$ | 0.75 |
| $\frac{1}{8}$ | 0.125 |
| $\frac{1}{16}$ | 0.062 |
| $\frac{1}{32}$ | 0.031 |
| $\frac{1}{3}$ | 0.333 |
| $\frac{2}{3}$ | 0.666 |

# Area

*To calculate the areas of different shapes use the following formulae:*

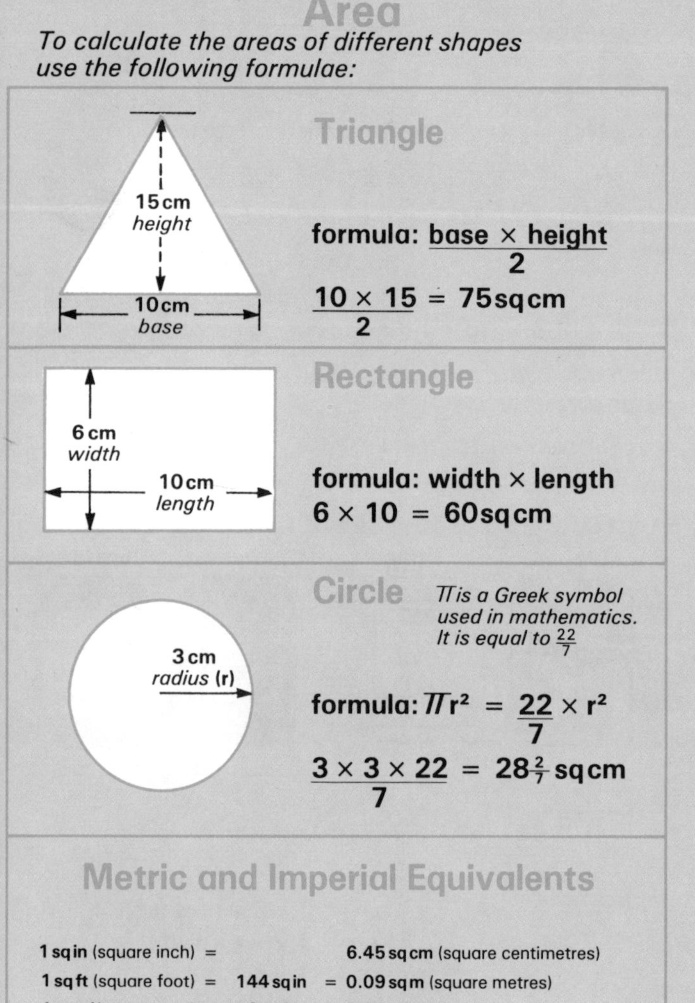


## Triangle

formula: $\frac{\text{base} \times \text{height}}{2}$

$\frac{10 \times 15}{2} = 75$ sq cm

## Rectangle

formula: width × length

$6 \times 10 = 60$ sq cm

## Circle

*$\pi$ is a Greek symbol used in mathematics. It is equal to $\frac{22}{7}$*

formula: $\pi r^2 = \frac{22}{7} \times r^2$

$\frac{3 \times 3 \times 22}{7} = 28\frac{2}{7}$ sq cm

## Metric and Imperial Equivalents

| | | | | |
|---|---|---|---|---|
| **1 sq in** (square inch) | = | | | **6.45 sq cm** (square centimetres) |
| **1 sq ft** (square foot) | = | **144 sq in** | = | **0.09 sq m** (square metres) |
| **1 sq yd** (square yard) | = | **9 sq ft** | = | **0.84 sq m** |
| **1 acre** | = | **4 840 sq yd** | = | **4046.72 sq m** |
| **1 sq mile** | = | **640 acres** | = | **258.9 hectares** |

# Weight: metric

| | | | |
|---|---|---|---|
| mg | 1000 milligrams | = | 1 gram |
| g | 1000 grams | = | 1 kilogram |
| kg | 100 kilograms | = | 1 quintal |
| | 10 quintals | = | 1 tonne |

*Use grams to buy sweets.*

*Use kilograms to buy flour, potatoes etc.*

*Use tonnes to buy coal.*

## Groceries

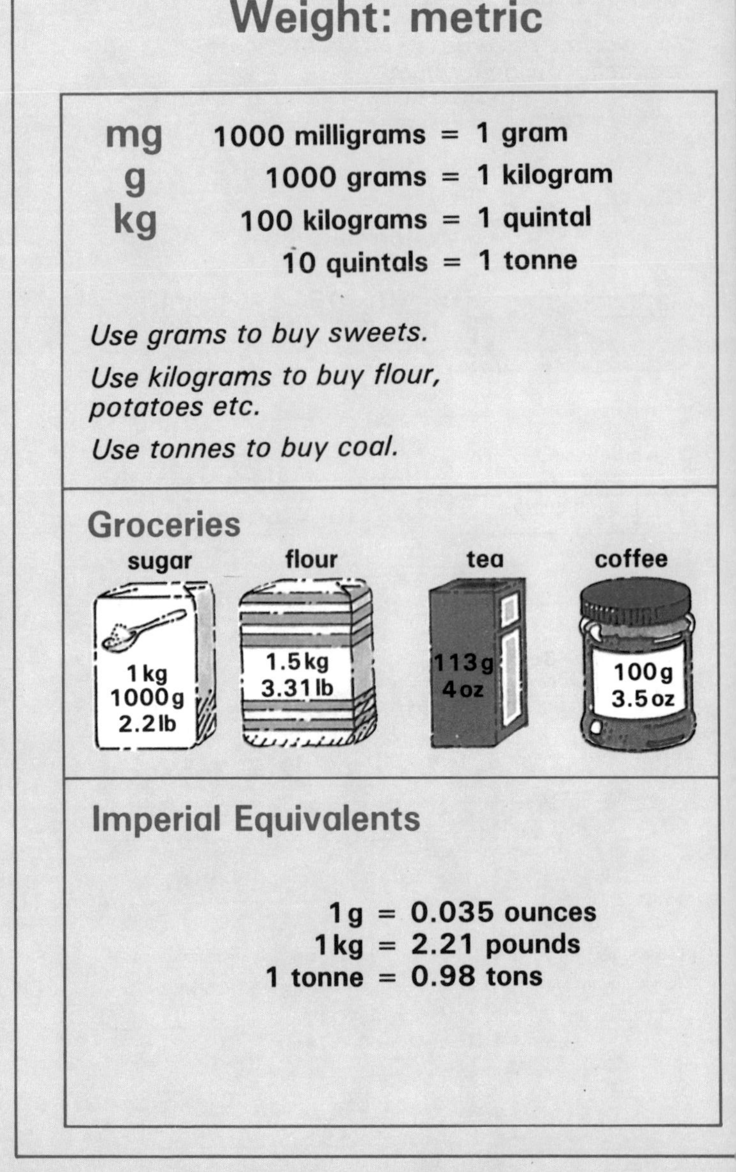


## Imperial Equivalents

1 g = 0.035 ounces
1 kg = 2.21 pounds
1 tonne = 0.98 tons

# Weight: imperial

| | |
|---|---|
| oz | 16 drams = 1 ounce |
| lb | 16 ounces = 1 pound |
| st | 14 pounds = 1 stone |
| qtr | 2 stones = 1 quarter |
| cwt | 4 quarters = 1 hundredweight |
| | 112 pounds = 1 cwt |
| | 20 cwt = 1 ton |

## Metric Equivalents

1 ounce = 28.35g

1 pound = 0.45kg

1 stone = 6.35kg

1 hundredweight = 50.8kg or 0.51 quintals

1 ton = 1.016 tonnes

# Length: metric

| | | |
|---|---|---|
| mm | **10 millimetres = 1 centimetre** | |
| cm | **10 centimetres = 1 decimetre** | |
| dm | **10 decimetres = 1 metre** | |
| m | **1000 metres = 1 kilometre** | km |

**The basic unit is a *metre*.**

**1 metre = 1000mm**<br>
**100cm**<br>
**10dm**

The metric system was introduced in 1791-95 and legally adopted in France in 1801. The change to the metric system began in the1970's in the UK.

The standard *metre* was to measure 1/10 000 000 of the distance from the North Pole to the Equator on a line passing through Paris.

The *litre* (liquid measure) was a cube with sides 1/10 of a metre.

A *gram* (dry measure) was 1/1000 of the weight of a litre of water at 4° centigrade.

# Length: imperial

in(″)
ft(′)
yd(ˣ)

| | | |
|---|---|---|
| 12 inches | = | 1 foot |
| 3 feet | = | 1 yard |
| 22 yards | = | 1 chain |
| 10 chains | = | 1 furlong |
| 8 furlongs | = | 1 mile |
| 1760 yards | = | 1 mile |
| 5280 feet | = | 1 mile |
| 63360 inches | = | 1 mile |

The basic unit of length is a yard. The standard yard was established in 1844 by a Royal Commission. In 1963 the Weights and Measures Act defined the following equivalents:

## Metric Equivalents

| | | |
|---|---|---|
| 1 yd | = | 0.91 m |
| 1 in | = | 25.4 mm or 2.54 cm |
| 1 mm | = | 0.04 in |
| 1 m | = | 1.09 yd or 3.28 ft |
| 1 km | = | 0.62 miles or approx $5/8$ mile |

# Capacity: metric

| | | | |
|---|---|---|---|
| ml | 10 millilitres | = | 1 centilitre |
| cl | 10 centilitres | = | 1 decilitre |
| dl | 10 decilitres | = | 1 litre |
| l | 10 litres | = | 1 decalitre |
| hl | 100 litres | = | 1 hectolitre |

## Imperial and Metric Equivalents

| | | |
|---|---|---|
| 1 pint | = | 0.568 litres<br>or 568 millilitres |
| 20 fluid oz | = | 1 pint |
| 1 gallon | = | 4.546 litres |
| 1 litre | = | 1.759 pints |

# Capacity: imperial

**fl oz**

20 fluid ounces = 1 pint
4 gills = 1 pint
2 pints = 1 quart
8 pints = 1 gallon
4 quarts = 1 gallon
2 gallons = 1 peck
9 gallons = 1 firkin
36 gallons = 1 barrel
4 pecks = 1 bushel

Wine
70 cl

MILK
1 pt
0.56 litres

OIL
35.2 fl oz
1 litre

# Roman Numerals

The Romans used letters to represent numbers. These numbers are still used and can be seen on monuments, buildings, clocks etc.

| | | | |
|---|---|---|---|
| 1 | I | 15 | XV |
| 2 | II | 16 | XVI |
| 3 | III | 17 | XVII |
| 4 | IV | 18 | XVIII |
| 5 | V | 19 | XIX |
| 6 | VI | 20 | XX |
| 7 | VII | 50 | L |
| 8 | VIII | 60 | LX |
| 9 | IX | 90 | XC |
| 10 | X | 100 | C |
| 11 | XI | 500 | D |
| 12 | XII | 900 | CM |
| 13 | XIII | 1000 | M |
| 14 | XIV | 1900 | MCM |

A line over a numeral multiplies it by 1000
e.g. $\overline{VI}$ = 6000

# Early Number Systems

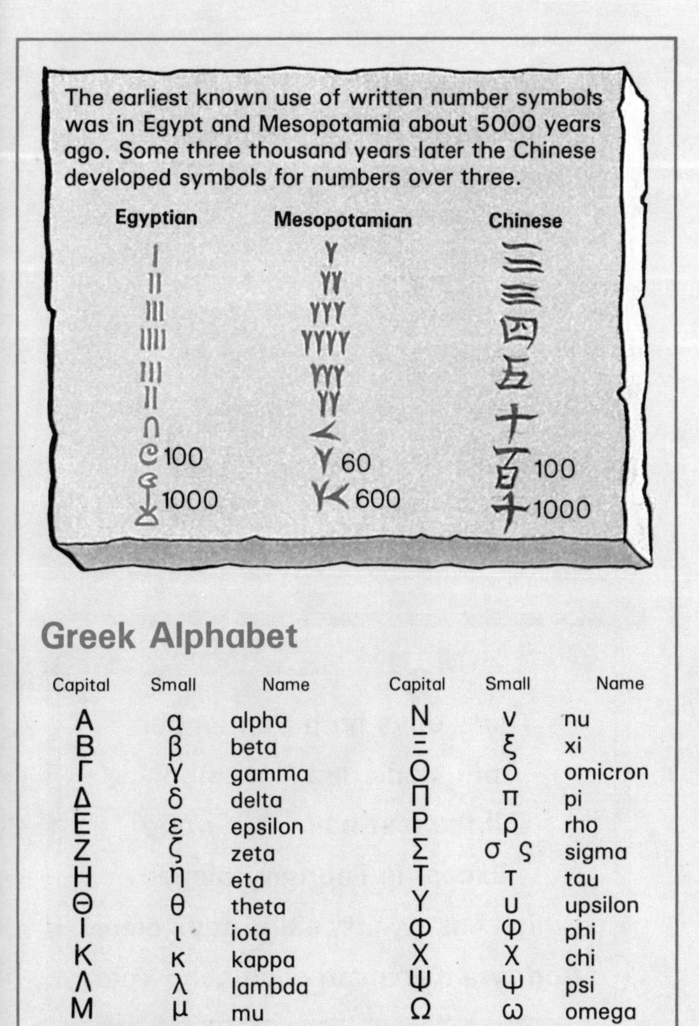


## Greek Alphabet

| Capital | Small | Name | Capital | Small | Name |
|---|---|---|---|---|---|
| Α | α | alpha | Ν | ν | nu |
| Β | β | beta | Ξ | ξ | xi |
| Γ | γ | gamma | Ο | ο | omicron |
| Δ | δ | delta | Π | π | pi |
| Ε | ε | epsilon | Ρ | ρ | rho |
| Ζ | ζ | zeta | Σ | σ ς | sigma |
| Η | η | eta | Τ | τ | tau |
| Θ | θ | theta | Υ | υ | upsilon |
| Ι | ι | iota | Φ | φ | phi |
| Κ | κ | kappa | Χ | χ | chi |
| Λ | λ | lambda | Ψ | ψ | psi |
| Μ | μ | mu | Ω | ω | omega |

# Time

| | | |
|---|---|---|
| 60 seconds | = | 1 minute |
| 60 minutes | = | 1 hour |
| 24 hours | = | 1 day |
| 7 days | = | 1 week |
| 4 weeks | = | 1 month |
| 12 months | = | 1 year |
| 365 days | = | 1 year |
| 366 days | = | 1 Leap year |
| 10 years | = | 1 decade |
| 100 years | = | 1 century |
| 1000 years | = | 1 millennium |

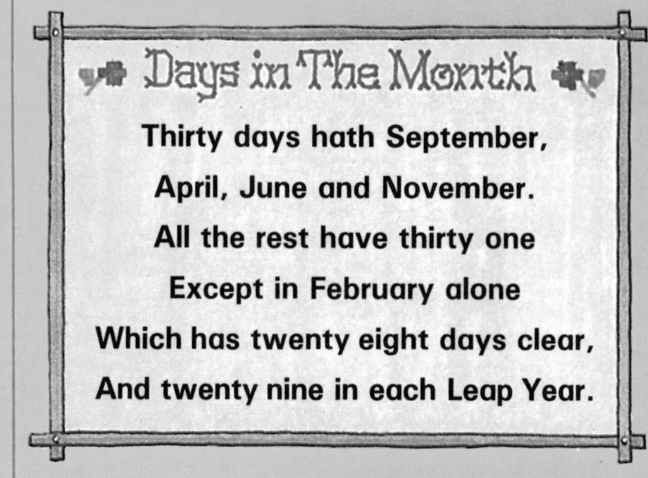

# Time

## Leap Years

Leap years occur every fourth year. To discover which is a leap year, divide the numbers of the year by four. In a leap year these numbers will divide evenly.
e.g. 1984, 1988, 1992, 1996, 2000 etc.

**Meridies is the Latin word for noon.**
**Ante means before : Post means after**

From midnight to before noon is morning = ante meridiem = a.m.

12 noon = midday

From noon to 12 midnight = afternoon = post meridiem = p.m.

# 24 Hour Clock

By bus, rail, sea or air, timetables are shown using the 24 hour clock. Digital clocks and watches display the time in this way.

**00.00 = 12 o'clock**
**or 24.00 midnight**

**12.00 = 12 o'clock midday**

**01.00 = 1 a.m.** **13.00 = 1 p.m.**

**02.00 = 2 a.m.** **14.00 = 2 p.m.**

**03.00 = 3 a.m.** **15.00 = 3 p.m.**

**04.00 = 4 a.m.** **16.00 = 4 p.m.**

**05.00 = 5 a.m.** **17.00 = 5 p.m.**

**06.00 = 6 a.m.** **18.00 = 6 p.m.**

**07.00 = 7 a.m.** **19.00 = 7 p.m.**

**08.00 = 8 a.m.** **20.00 = 8 p.m.**

**09.00 = 9 a.m.** **21.00 = 9 p.m.**

**10.00 = 10 a.m.** **22.00 = 10 p.m.**

**11.00 = 11 a.m.** **23.00 = 11 p.m.**

# World Times

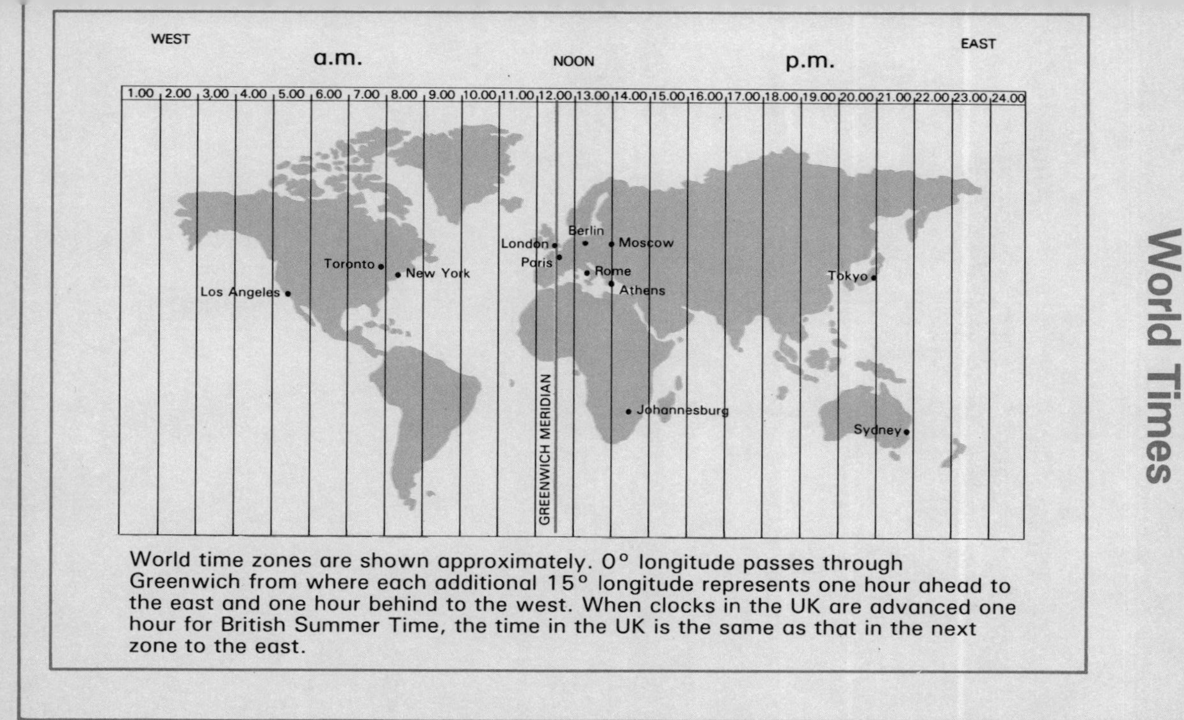


World time zones are shown approximately. 0° longitude passes through Greenwich from where each additional 15° longitude represents one hour ahead to the east and one hour behind to the west. When clocks in the UK are advanced one hour for British Summer Time, the time in the UK is the same as that in the next zone to the east.

# Temperatures

## C° Celsius or Centigrade

**To convert to Fahrenheit:**

$\times 9 \div 5 + 32$

*(Named after Anders Celsius 1701-1744, Swedish astronomer)*

## F° Fahrenheit

**To convert to Centigrade:**

$- 32 \times 5 \div 9$

*(Named after Gabriel Fahrenheit 1686-1736, German physicist)*

| | °C | °F | |
|---|---|---|---|
| | 120 | 240 | |
| | 110 | 230 | |
| | | 220 | |
| 100°C water boils (at sea level) | 100 | 210 | 212°F water boils (at sea level) |
| | | 200 | |
| | 90 | 190 | |
| | 80 | 180 | |
| | | 170 | |
| | 70 | 160 | |
| | | 150 | |
| | 60 | 140 | |
| | | 130 | |
| | 50 | 120 | |
| | | 110 | |
| | 40 | 100 | |
| 36.9°C body temperature | | | 98.4°F body temperature |
| | 30 | 90 | |
| | | 80 | |
| | 20 | 70 | |
| | | 60 | |
| | 10 | 50 | |
| | | 40 | |
| 0°C water freezes (at sea level) | 0 | 30 | 32°F water freezes (at sea level) |
| | | 20 | |
| | 10 | 10 | |
| | 20 | 0 | |
| | | 10 | |

# Oven Temperatures

| Gas Mark | Electricity C° | F° | Heat of oven |
|---|---|---|---|
| 1 | 120 | 250 | |
| 2 | 150 | 300 | slow |
| 3 | 170 | 325 | very moderate |
| 4 | 180 | 350 | moderate |
| 5 | 190 | 375 | moderately hot |
| 6 | 200 | 400 | |
| 7 | 220 | 425 | hot |
| 8 | 230 | 450 | |
| 9 | 260 | 500 | very hot |

# Beaufort Wind Scale

| *Beaufort Number* | *Wind* | *mph* | *kph* | *Effect over land* |
|---|---|---|---|---|
| 0 | Calm | 1 | 1.6 | *Smoke rises vertically* |
| 1 | Light air | 1–3 | 1.6–5 | *Smoke drifts* |
| 2 | Light breeze | 4–7 | 6–11 | *Leaves rustle, wind felt on face* |
| 3 | Gentle breeze | 8–12 | 13–19 | *Leaves move, light flag is extended* |
| 4 | Moderate breeze | 13–18 | 21–29 | *Dust and loose paper blows about. Small branches move* |
| 5 | Fresh breeze | 19–24 | 30–39 | *Small trees sway a little* |
| 6 | Strong breeze | 25–31 | 40–50 | *Large branches sway, wires whistle* |
| 7 | Moderate gale | 32–38 | 51–61 | *Whole trees sway, hard to walk against the wind* |
| 8 | Fresh gale | 39–46 | 63–74 | *Twigs break off trees, very hard to walk into wind* |
| 9 | Strong gale | 47–54 | 75–87 | *Chimney pots and slates blown off. Large branches down* |
| 10 | Whole gale | 55–63 | 88–101 | *Trees uprooted, serious damage to buildings* |
| 11 | Storm | 64–72 | 103–115 | *Very rare inland, causes widespread damage* |
| 12 | Hurricane | 73 and more | 116 and more | *Disastrous results* |

In 1955, the US Weather Bureau added numbers 13 to 17 to the scale. These numbers represent hurricanes with wind speeds of up to 136 mph (219 kph).

## Fabric widths

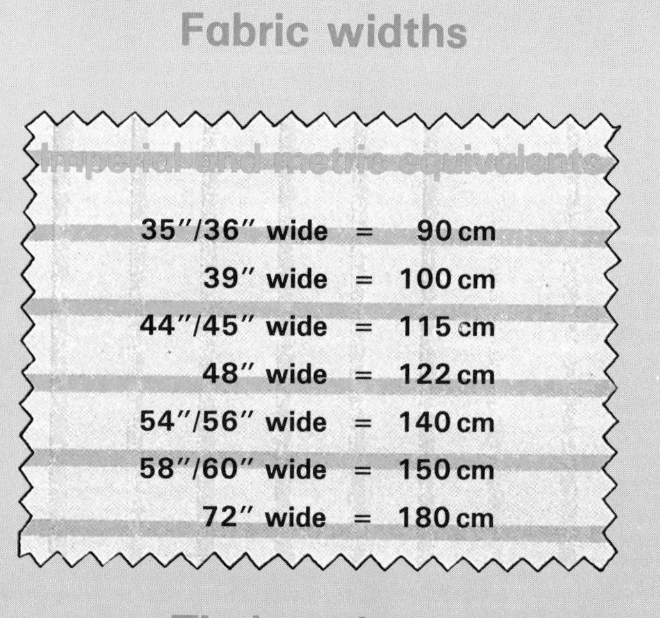


| | | |
|---|---|---|
| 35″/36″ wide | = | 90 cm |
| 39″ wide | = | 100 cm |
| 44″/45″ wide | = | 115 cm |
| 48″ wide | = | 122 cm |
| 54″/56″ wide | = | 140 cm |
| 58″/60″ wide | = | 150 cm |
| 72″ wide | = | 180 cm |

## Timber sizes

| | | | |
|---|---|---|---|
| $\frac{3}{16}$″ | = 4 mm | $\frac{5}{8}$″ | = 15 mm |
| $\frac{1}{4}$″ | = 6 mm | $\frac{3}{4}$″ | = 18 mm |
| $\frac{3}{8}$″ | = 9 mm | 1″ | = 25 mm |
| $\frac{1}{2}$″ | = 12 mm | $1\frac{1}{4}$″ | = 30 mm |
| 1.8 m | = 5′ $10\frac{7}{8}$″ | 3.9 m | = 12′ $9\frac{1}{2}$″ |
| 2.1 m | = 6′ $10\frac{5}{8}$″ | 4.2 m | = 13′ $9\frac{3}{8}$″ |
| 2.4 m | = 7′ $10\frac{1}{2}$″ | 4.5 m | = 14′ $9\frac{1}{8}$″ |
| 2.7 m | = 8′ $10\frac{1}{4}$″ | 4.8 m | = 15′ 9″ |
| 3.0 m | = 9′ $10\frac{1}{8}$″ | 5.1 m | = 16′ $8\frac{3}{4}$″ |
| 3.3 m | = 10′ $9\frac{7}{8}$″ | 5.4 m | = 17′ $8\frac{5}{8}$″ |
| 3.6 m | = 11′ $9\frac{3}{4}$″ | 5.7 m | = 18′ $8\frac{3}{4}$″ |

# Earth

The earth has an Equatorial circumference of 24,901.47 miles (40,075.03 km) but a Polar circumference of 24,859.75 miles (40,007.89 km). It is not a true sphere but is flattened at the Poles and therefore called an *ellipsoid*.

Approximately ⅔ of the earth's surface is covered in salt water. The Pacific Ocean is nearly 20% greater than Earth's total land area.

The world population exceeds 4,000,000,000 and grows by 100,000,000 per year.

## Distances from Earth and Sun (in miles)

| Planet | Distances from Earth: Maximum | Distances from Earth: Minimum | Distance from Sun |
|---|---|---|---|
| **Mercury** | **136,900,000** | **49,100,000** | **36,000,000** |
| **Venus** | **160,900,000** | **25,700,000** | **67,200,000** |
| **Mars** | **247,000,000** | **34,000,000** | **141,500,000** |
| **Jupiter** | **597,000,000** | **362,000,000** | **483,300,000** |
| **Saturn** | **1,023,000,000** | **773,000,000** | **886,100,000** |
| **Uranus** | **1,946,000,000** | **1,594,000,000** | **1,783,000,000** |
| **Neptune** | **2,891,000,000** | **2,654,000,000** | **2,793,000,000** |
| **Pluto** | **4,506,000,000** | **2,605,000,000** | **3,674,000,000** |

*The Earth's distance from the sun is 92,868,000 miles*

# Geological Table

| Era | Period | Period lasted for *(millions of year* |
|---|---|---|
| **Cenozoic** (Quaternary) | Holocene<br>Pleistocene | about 0.2 |
| **Cenozoic** (Tertiary) | Pliocene | 5 |
| | Miocene | 19 |
| | Oligocene | 12 |
| | Eocene | 16 |
| | Palaeocene | 11 |
| **Mesozoic** | Cretaceous | 70 |
| | Jurassic | 60 |
| | Triassic | 30 |
| **Palaeozoic** | Permian | 55 |
| | Carboniferous | 65 |
| | Devonian | 50 |
| | Silurian | 45 |
| | Ordovician | 60 |
| | Cambrian | 70 |
| **Proterozoic** | Pre-Cambrian | about 1430 |
| **Azoic** | | about 2600 |

| Number of Years ago *(in millions)* | Distinct forms of Life |
|---|---|
| about 2 | Man, woman and plants and animals we see today. Ice-age – many plants and animals died out.  |
| 7<br>26<br>38<br>54<br>65 | Modernized mammals.<br>Primitive apes.<br>Flowering plants and grasses.<br>Earliest form of horse.  |
| 135<br>195<br>225 | Dinosaurs die out.<br>Age of reptiles, ammonites and belemnites.<br>Earliest dinosaurs and mammals.  |
| 280<br>345<br>395<br>440<br>500<br>570 | Pteridosperms dominant.<br>Rise of amphibians.<br>Rise of fish and land plants such as ferns.<br>Age of graptolites, trilobites and many other invertebrates.<br>Plant life in the sea.  |
| about 2000<br>4600 | Extremely rare traces of life, algae from at least 1,700 million years ago.<br>The beginnings of life in the sea. 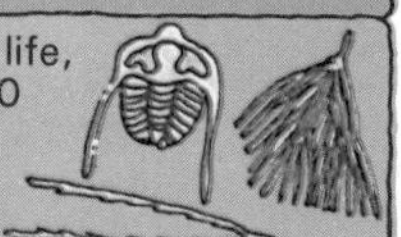 |

# Comparative Clothing Sizes

*(This is only a rough guide as sizes vary between manufacturers)*

## Shirts

| | | | | | | | | | | | | |
|---|---|---|---|---|---|---|---|---|---|---|---|---|
| **U K/U S A** inches | 12 | 12½ | 13 | 13½ | 14 | 14½ | 15 | 15½ | 16 | 16½ | 17 | 17½ |
| **U K/Europe** centimetres | 30·31 | 32 | 33 | 34·35 | 36 | 37 | 38 | 39·40 | 41 | 42 | 43 | 44·45 |

## Ladies Clothes

| | | | | | | | |
|---|---|---|---|---|---|---|---|
| **U K** size code | 10 | 12 | 14 | 16 | 18 | 20 | 22 |
| Bust/hip – inches | 32/34 | 34/36 | 36/38 | 38/40 | 40/42 | 42/44 | 44/46 |
| Bust/hip – centimetres | 84/89 | 88/93 | 92/97 | 97/102 | 102/107 | 107/112 | 112/117 |
| **U S A** size code | 10 | 12 | 14 | 16 | 18 | 20 | 22 |
| Bust/hip – inches | 33/35 | 34½/36½ | 36/38 | 37½/39½ | 39/41 | 41/43 | 43/45 |

*(European sizes vary from country to country)*

## Children's Clothes

| | | | | | | | | | | | | |
|---|---|---|---|---|---|---|---|---|---|---|---|---|
| **UK** Age | 1 | 2 | 3 | 4 | 5 | 6 | 7 | 8 | 9 | 10 | 11 | 12 |
| Height – inches | 32 | 36 | 38 | 40 | 43 | 45 | 48 | 50 | 53 | 55 | 58 | 60 |
| centimetres | 80 | 92 | 98 | 104 | 110 | 116 | 122 | 128 | 134 | 140 | 146 | 152 |
| **U S A** Boys' size code | 1 | 2 | 3 | 4 | 5 | 6 | 8 | | 10 | | 12 | |
| Girls' size code | 2 | 3 | 4 | 5 | 6 | 6x | 7 | 8 | 10 | | 12 | |
| **Europe** Height – centimetres | 80 | 92 | 98 | 104 | 110 | 116 | 122 | 128 | 134 | 140 | 146 | 152 |

# Comparative Shoe Sizes

*(All sizes are approximate)*

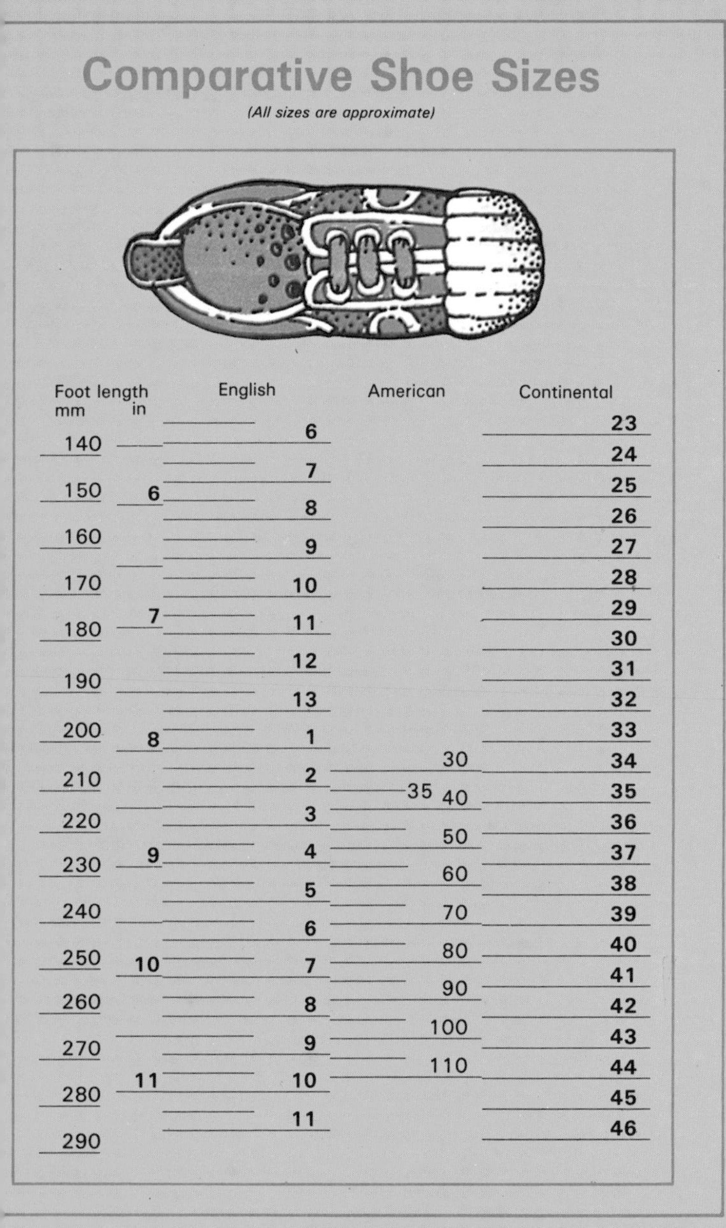

# Washing Instructions

| Code | Machine | Hand |
|---|---|---|
| 1 95° | Very hot to boiling<br>Maximum wash | Hand hot or boiling |
| | SPIN OR WRING | |
|  | Hot maximum wash | Hand hot |
| | SPIN OR WRING | |
|  | Hot medium wash | Hand hot |
| | Cold rinse: short spin or drip dry | |
|  | Hand hot: medium wash | Hand hot |
| | Cold rinse: short spin or drip dry | |
|  | Warm: maximum wash | Warm |
| | SPIN OR WRING | |
| 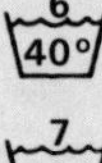 | Warm: minimum wash<br>Cold rinse | Warm<br>Short spin |
| | DO NOT WRING | |
|  | Warm: minimum wash | Warm: do not rub |
| | SPIN: DO NOT HAND WRING | |
|  | Cool: minimum wash | Cool |
| | Cold rinse short spin<br>DO NOT WRING | |
|  | | HANDWASH: See instructions on garment label |
| | DO NOT MACHINE OR HAND WASH | |

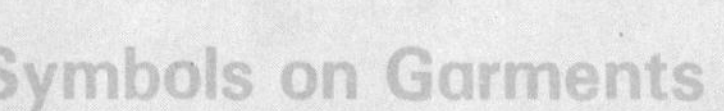

## Symbols on Garments

**Do not bleach**

**Dry cleanable**

**Ironing instructions**

**Not dry-cleanable**

**LOOK AT GARMENT LABELS BEFORE WASHING OR IRONING**

# World Currencies

| *Country* | *Currency* |
|---|---|
| ALGERIA | dinar |
| AUSTRALIA | dollars |
| AUSTRIA | schillings |
| CANADA | dollars |
| DENMARK | kroner |
| EGYPT | Egyptian pounds |
| EIRE | Irish pounds (punts) |
| FRANCE | francs |
| GERMANY | Deutschmarks |
| GHANA | çedi |
| GREAT BRITAIN | pounds sterling |
| GREECE | drachma |
| HONG KONG | dollars |
| INDIA | rupees |
| ITALY | lire |
| JAPAN | yen |
| KENYA | shillings |
| KUWAIT | dinar |
| LEBANON | pounds |
| MALAYSIA | ringgits (Malaysian dollars) |
| MALTA | Maltese pounds |
| MEXICO | pesos |
| MOROCCO | dirham |
| NETHERLANDS | guilders |
| NEW ZEALAND | dollars |
| NIGERIA | naira |
| PAKISTAN | rupees |
| PHILIPPINES | pesos |
| PORTUGAL | escudos |
| SAUDI ARABIA | riyals |
| SINGAPORE | dollars |
| SOUTH AFRICA | rand |
| SPAIN | pesetas |
| TUNISIA | dinar |
| TURKEY | liras |
| USA | dollars |
| ZAIRE | zaire |

# Signs, symbols & abbreviations

| | | | |
|---|---|---|---|
| $=$ | is equal to | cm | centimetre(s) |
| $\neq$ | is not equal to | mm | millimetre(s) |
| $\fallingdotseq$ | is approx equal to | m | metre(s) |
| $\equiv$ | is identical to | km | kilometre(s) |
| $\ngtr$ | not greater than | mg | milligram(s) |
| $>$ | greater than | gm | gram(s) |
| $<$ | less than | kg | kilogram(s) |
| $\nless$ | not less than | ml | millilitre(s) |
| $\sum$ | the sum of | cl | centilitre(s) |
| $\angle$ | angle | l | litre(s) |
| $\infty$ | infinity | sq | square |
| $\in$ | is a member of the set of | cu | cubic |
| $\notin$ | is not a member of the set of | oz | ounce |
| $\therefore$ | therefore | lb | pound |
| $\because$ | because | cwt | hundred-weight |
| | | in/″ | inches |
| | | ft/′ | feet |
| | | yd/$^{x}$ | yards |

# Historical Measures

| Measure | Imperial | Metric |
|---|---|---|
| *Length* | | |
| digit | 0.729 in | 1.85 cm |
| nail | 2.25 in | 5.63 cm |
| hand (width) | 4 in | 10.16 cm |
| palm (length) | 8 in | 20.3 cm |
| span | 9 in | 22.8 cm |
| foot | 12 in | 30.1 cm |
| cubit | 18 – 22 in | c.53 cm |
| pace | 30 in | 76.2 cm |
| fathom (4 cubits) | 72 in | 182.9 cm |
| stadium | 202 yd | 184.7 m |
| Roman mile (1000 paces) | 1611 yd | 1473 m |
| *Weight* | | |
| grain (smallest unit) | $\frac{1}{7000}$ lb | 0.064 g |
| dram | 27.34 grains | |
| 16 drams | 1 oz | 28.35 g |
| 1 pennyweight | 24 grains | 15.55 g |
| peck | 2 gallons (dry goods) | 9.092 litres |
| bushel | 4 pecks | 36.37 litres |
| firkin | 9 gallons | 40.91 litres |
| barrel | 36 gallons | 163.65 litres |
| shipload | 421 tons | 427.75 tonnes |
| *Money* | | |
| talent (Greek, Roman, Assyrian) | | £243.75* |
| groat (Old English) | 4d | $1\frac{1}{2}$p* |

**This is the face value of these coins, not their worth today*

# Interesting Number Facts

If a man could jump as well as a flea, he would be able to jump over St Paul's Cathedral: 110 m or 365 ft.

The world's heaviest man died in 1958, weighing 485 kg (1069 lbs) or 76 st 5 lbs.

A blind person using Braille needs 1 hour to 'read' 3000 words.

A daily newspaper may contain 100,000 words (not including adverts), equal to a 200 page novel.